For Elin
S.W.

ORCHARD BOOKS
338 Euston Road, London NW1 3BH
Hachette Children's Books
Level 17/207, Kent Street, Sydney, NSW 2000
ISBN 1 84362 525 3 (hardback)
ISBN 1 84362 533 4 (paperback)
First published in Great Britain in 2005
First paperback publication in 2006
Text © Tony Bradman 2005 Illustrations © Sarah Warburton 2005
The rights of Tony Bradman to be identified as the author
and of Sarah Warburton to be identified as the illustrator of this
work have been asserted by them in accordance with the Copyright,
Designs and Patents Act, 1988. A CIP catalogue record for this book is
available from the British Library.
1 3 5 7 9 10 8 6 4 2 (hardback)
3 5 7 9 10 8 6 4 (paperback)

Tony Bradman

Happy Ever After

RAPUNZEL
CUTS LOOSE

Illustrated by Sarah Warburton

ORCHARD BOOKS

It was Saturday, and Rapunzel and her husband, Prince Dynamo, were having breakfast together at the palace. He was tucking into his third bowl of royal cereal, but Rapunzel had barely touched her muesli.

"Lost your appetite, my love?" said Prince
Dynamo. "What's wrong?"

"Oh, er...nothing much," said
Rapunzel. She sighed. "I just don't like
Saturdays, that's all."

"Really?" said Prince Dynamo, surprised. "What's not to like? I *love* Saturdays. I can spend the whole day doing the things I enjoy. It's golf this morning, tennis this afternoon, a fencing match this evening..."

"In case you've forgotten," said
Rapunzel. "Saturday is the day I wash
my hair."

They both looked at the shining river
of golden tresses that flowed from
Rapunzel's head, down her back, onto
the floor and round the table.

Twelve servants stood by to carry it,
like the train of a dress.

Twelve more servants were needed to brush it, which usually took from breakfast till lunch.

And as for washing it, well, Rapunzel knew she'd be spending *her* Saturday in The Royal Bathroom.

Teams of servants would use enough water to float a ship, and several huge vats of shampoo.

Then drying her hair would take
till after midnight. The electricity bills
were enormous.

She hated the whole business, and so did the royal hairdresser.

He was always complaining that he never had anything interesting to do with her hair.

"I don't understand," said Prince Dynamo. "Is washing your hair a problem?"

"Well, yes," Rapunzel said nervously. "In fact, I've, er, been thinking of getting my hair cut."

"You can't do that!" said Prince Dynamo, looking upset. "I love your long hair. It's what brought me to you in the first place!"

Rapunzel frowned. She'd had a feeling this was going to be difficult.

Ever since Rapunzel had let down her hair from a window, and the prince had climbed up it to rescue her from the wicked witch, he had been going on about her lovely, long locks.

"But it's a real pain," said Rapunzel. "I'd love to play golf and tennis, and fence like you. I can't though, can I?"

"But I don't want you to change," said
the prince. "I just want you to be what
you are now...beautiful. Perfect. With
lovely, long hair. Besides, there's no
point in you taking up any sports. You'd
be useless at them."

"Excuse me?" said a shocked
Rapunzel.

"Oh, everybody knows girls are
rubbish at sport," Prince Dynamo said.

"Mind you, I'm beginning to think the
boys in the forest aren't too hot either.
None of them are good enough to beat
me. I can't seem to find anyone to give
me a decent game. Yikes, is that the
time? Must dash...bye!"

The prince grabbed a piece of toast, blew her a kiss, and left.

Rapunzel sat there scowling. So girls were rubbish at sport, were they? How dare he!

She had a good mind to summon the
royal hairdresser this instant and order
him to cut her hair off immediately.
Then she'd show the prince a thing
or two...

Although that might not be such
a great idea, Rapunzel realised. The
prince would probably make a fuss, and
want her to grow it back again. Besides,
she loved him really, even if he was
a ninny. She just had to find a way to
make them both happy...

In fact, what she needed was a plan...
Rapunzel thought hard while her hair
was being washed, but she didn't come
up with much.

After a while, she picked up
a magazine out of sheer boredom and
read an article about wigs. Now that's
interesting, Rapunzel thought...

By Monday morning, Rapunzel had her plan. She waited till the prince left the palace for a game of squash and then she summoned the royal hairdresser.

"How may I serve you today, Your Majesty?" he said, sounding bored already. "Some advice on shampoo? A change of hairbrush, perhaps?"

"Actually, I was thinking of asking you to do something rather, er... creative," said Rapunzel.

The Royal Hairdresser raised
an eyebrow.

So Rapunzel took a deep breath...and
told him her plan.

"Well, what do you think?" she said when she'd finished. "Are you up for it?"

"You can definitely count me in," he said, grinning. He pulled out his mobile and started dialling. "I've got some friends who'll be useful, too."

And thus began the transformation of Rapunzel. First, the royal hairdresser cut off her long hair. "Are you absolutely sure?" he asked.

"Do it," said Rapunzel.
SNIP! SNIP! SNIP!
"It's funky, it's modern, it's just so you," said the royal hairdresser when he'd finished.

Next, he and his team made a wig from the left-over hair. "It's a creative triumph," murmured the royal hairdresser, "even though I do say so myself!"

And finally, the royal hairdressing team made her a costume, a very special one...

But Rapunzel wasn't ready to put the
last part of her plan into operation yet.
She did lots of secret sporty training
first. She worked out at the gym...

She pounded the streets...

She practised all the prince's favourite
sports. Nobody recognised her with her
funky new hairstyle, of course.

But she always made sure she was
back at the palace - and wearing the
wig - well before the prince came home.

And soon she was ready. The
moment had come at last...

One morning, a few days later, Prince Dynamo was on the royal golf course with some friends, about to start a game. Suddenly, a strange, masked figure leapt out from behind a bush and stood before him.

"Hold it right there, Princey Baby," growled the figure. "I am, er...the Masked Mystery Girl, and I challenge you to a golf match. What do you say?"

"Play a girl?" said Prince Dynamo, laughing and looking round at his pals. "I don't think so. Now, would you mind..."

"Scared I'll beat you?" said the
Masked Mystery Girl.

"Why, you cheeky..." spluttered Prince
Dynamo. "Right, you're on. And I'll
beat you hands down...FORE!"

But the Prince didn't beat the Masked
Mystery Girl. He didn't get close. She
beat him...easily.

The prince immediately challenged her to a game of something else, so they played tennis. She beat him easily at that, too.

Then she beat him at squash, bowling, badminton, fencing, horse racing, running, archery, swimming, arm-wrestling...

Then she beat him at darts and chess.

She even beat him at Snap.

"That's it, I give up!" Prince Dynamo groaned. He was exhausted, and pretty bewildered as well. "I don't believe it. Who *are* you?"

The Masked Mystery Girl smiled, then whipped off her mask.

"But...but..." spluttered the prince. "Rapunzel - your hair! I mean, you look..." Rapunzel waited for him to finish, her heart beating fast. What if he hated it?

"You look absolutely fantastic!" he said.
And so Prince Dynamo fell in love with
Rapunzel all over again.

From that day on they played lots of sports together. The Prince admitted he'd been wrong about girls and sport... especially as he still found it hard to beat Rapunzel.

And Rapunzel changed her hairstyle more often than the prince changed his socks, which meant the royal hairdresser had plenty to keep him busy.

So we can be sure that Rapunzel and Prince Dynamo did live...
HAPPILY EVER AFTER!

Happy Ever After

Written by Tony Bradman
Illustrated by Sarah Warburton

Mr Wolf Bounces Back	1 84362 531 8	£3.99
Jack's Bean Snacks	1 84362 532 6	£3.99
Rapunzel Cuts Loose	1 84362 533 4	£3.99
Cinderella and the Mean Queen	1 84362 534 2	£3.99
The Frog Prince Hops to It	1 84362 535 0	£3.99
Red Riding Hood Takes Charge	1 84362 536 9	£3.99
Fairy Godmother Takes a Break	1 84362 537 7	£3.99
Goldilocks and the Just Right Club	1 84362 538 5	£3.99

These books are available from all good bookshops, or can be ordered direct
from the publisher: Orchard Books, PO BOX 29, Douglas IM99 1BQ.
Credit card orders please telephone 01624 836000 or fax 01624 837033 or
visit our Internet site: www.wattspub.co.uk or
e-mail: bookshop@enterprise.net for details.

To order please quote title, author and ISBN and your full name and
address. Cheques and postal orders should be made payable to 'Bookpost
plc.' Postage and packing is FREE within the UK
(overseas customers should add £1.00 per book).

Prices and availability are subject to change.